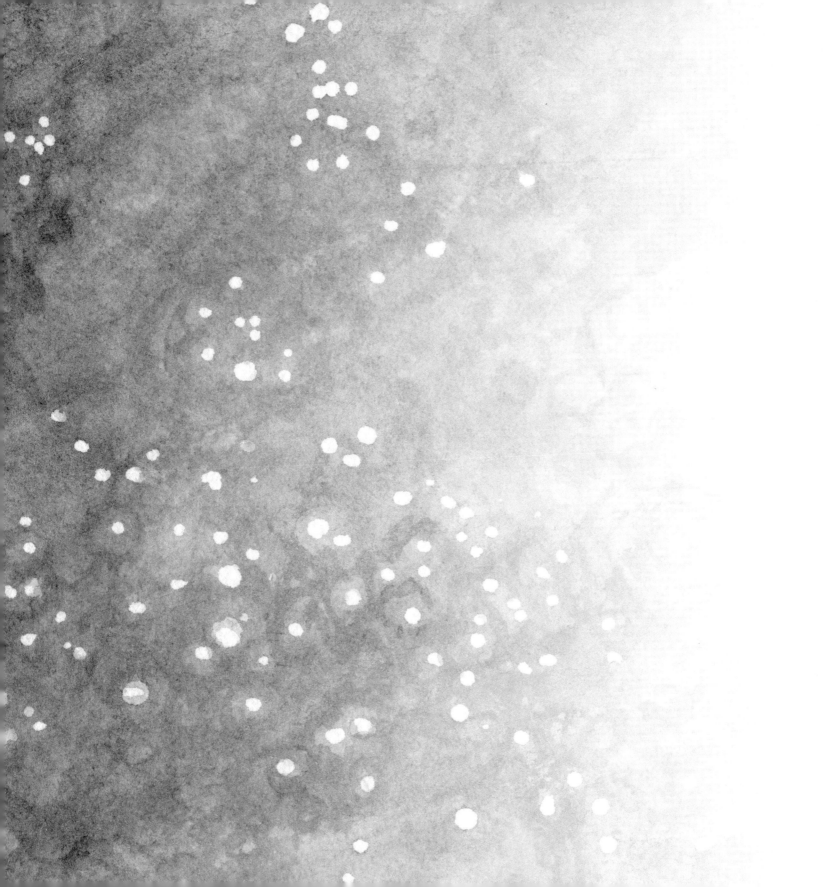

I Know You're Here

Krista Betcher

illustrated by Kari Vick

Kari Vick

Beaver's Pond Press

For CJ and Kyle, who
have shown me that our hearts
can still smile while grieving.
I'm blessed to be your mom.

-KB

For my steadfast husband,
Jim, and daughters, Kjersti &
Solveig. You are my earthly,
infinite treasure.

-KV

Edited by Hanna Kjeldbjerg
Illustrated by Kari Vick

ISBN 13: 978-1-59298-634-7

Library of Congress Catalog Number: 2018907555

Printed in Canada
First Printing: 2018

22 21 20 19 18   5 4 3 2 1

Book design and typesetting by Kevin Cannon

Beaver's Pond Press, Inc.
7108 Ohms Lane
Edina, MN 55439-2129
(952) 829-8818
www.BeaversPondPress.com

To order, visit www.ItascaBooks.com
or call (800) 901-3480. Reseller discounts available.

Contact Krista Betcher at www.KristaBetcher.com for school visits,
speaking engagements, freelance writing projects, and interviews.

A Message from the Author

I Know You're Here is a compilation of moments in time during the first three years after my husband's death. God Winks. Precious memories. Times when something hit me emotionally so hard that it stopped me in my tracks.

When I started photographing those times, it was so I could go back and remember those cherished memories. Never did I dream that my treasured photos would be transformed into something I could share with others.

This book is not mine alone, and I have many people to thank for helping my vision become a reality. Thank you to:

Cindy Boyum, my life coach, for helping me find my "new" self. I am forever grateful.

Hanna Kjeldbjerg, my editor, for her encouragement and patience.

Kari Vick, my illustrator, for her artistic inspiration. I'm blessed that she is my illustrator and also my friend.

Kevin Cannon, book designer extraordinaire, for his creative expertise.

Finally, reader: this book is for you. I hope you find moments of peace as you explore this book and reminisce about your loved ones.

In the blink
of an eye,
you were gone.

How does my heart know
you're
still
here?

When a spider web
sparkles in the
morning dew,

I know
you're here.

When the
silent deer
watches me
from across
the pond,

I know
you're
here.

When a
delicate
butterfly

flutters
from
flower to
flower,

I know
you're
here.

When the
sun's golden
rays

burst
through
a broken
cloud,

I know
you're
here.

When the cascading waterfall
leaves gentle drops
on my face,

I know you're here.

When a
hummingbird's
wings sing
as he hovers,

I know
you're
here.

When the
receding wave
reveals a
heart-shaped rock,

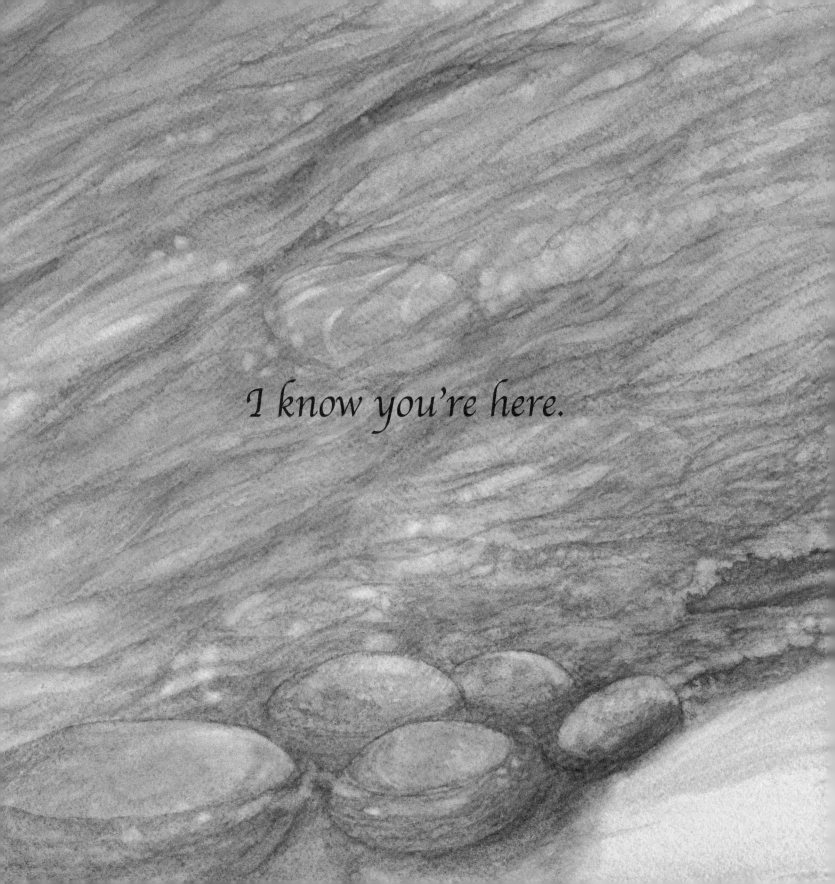

I know you're here.

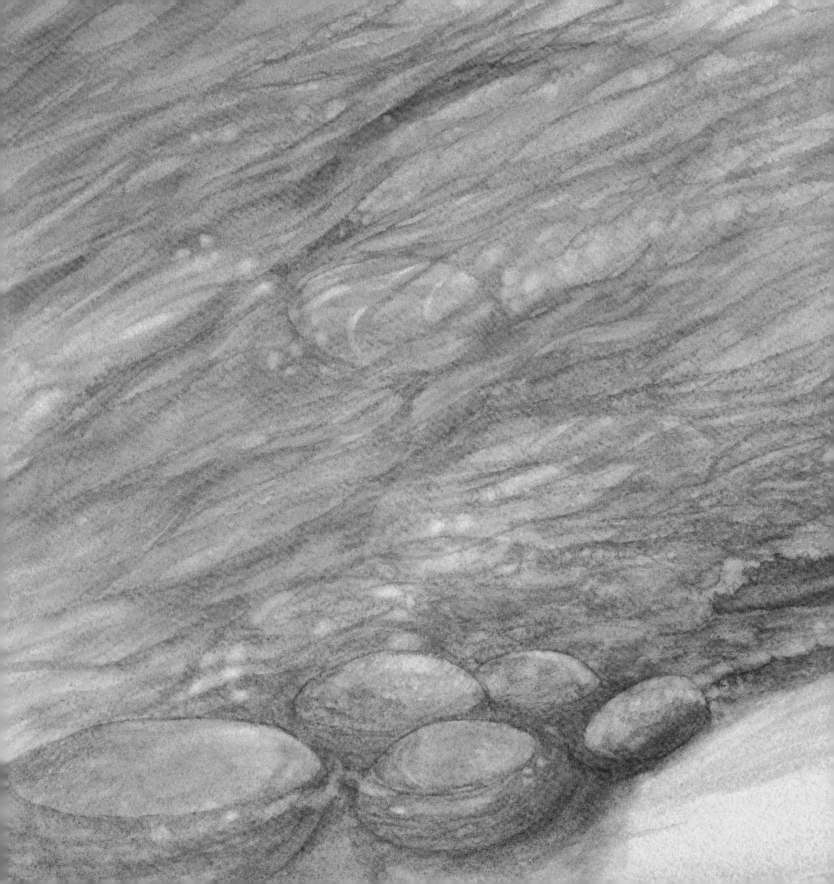

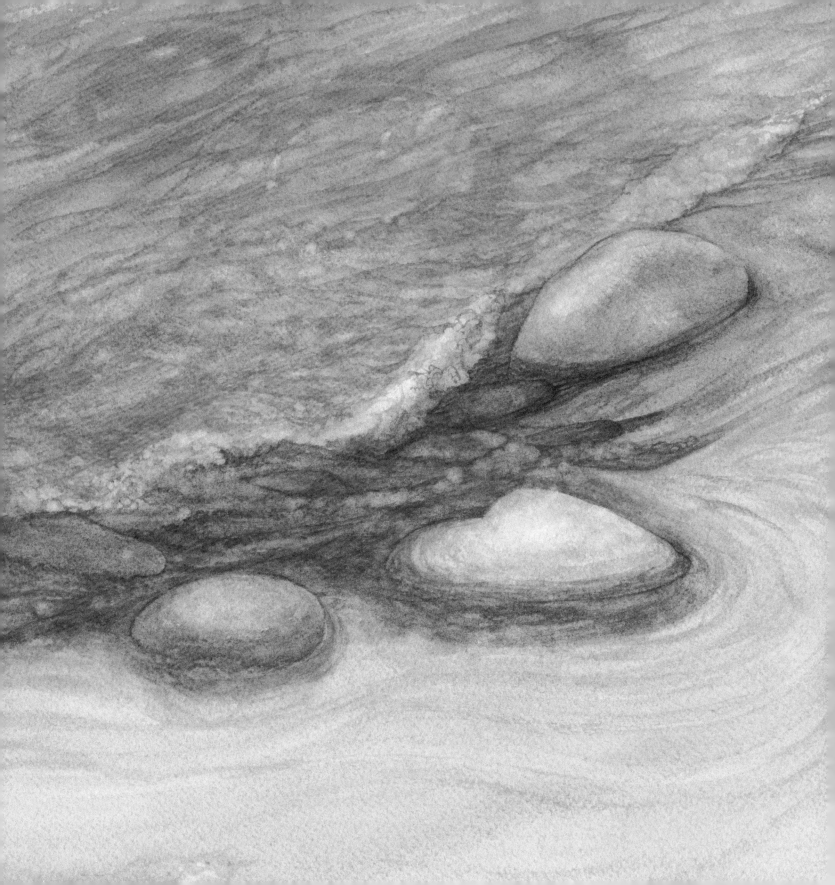

When
autumn leaves
tumble gently
to the
forest floor,

I know you're here.

When an eagle
circles above me
in the clear blue sky,

I know
you're here.

When a
rainbow
emerges
after the
passing
rain,

I know
you're
here.

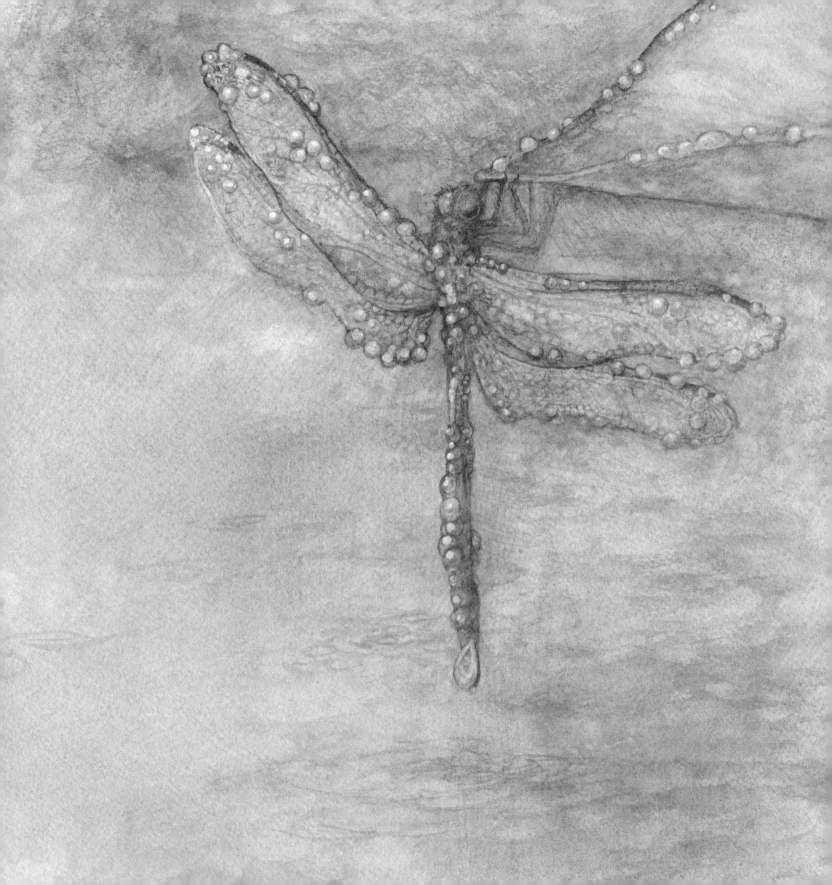

When a bright
red cardinal
appears among
the birch trees,

I know
you're here.

When a lingering sunset glows
across the distant horizon,

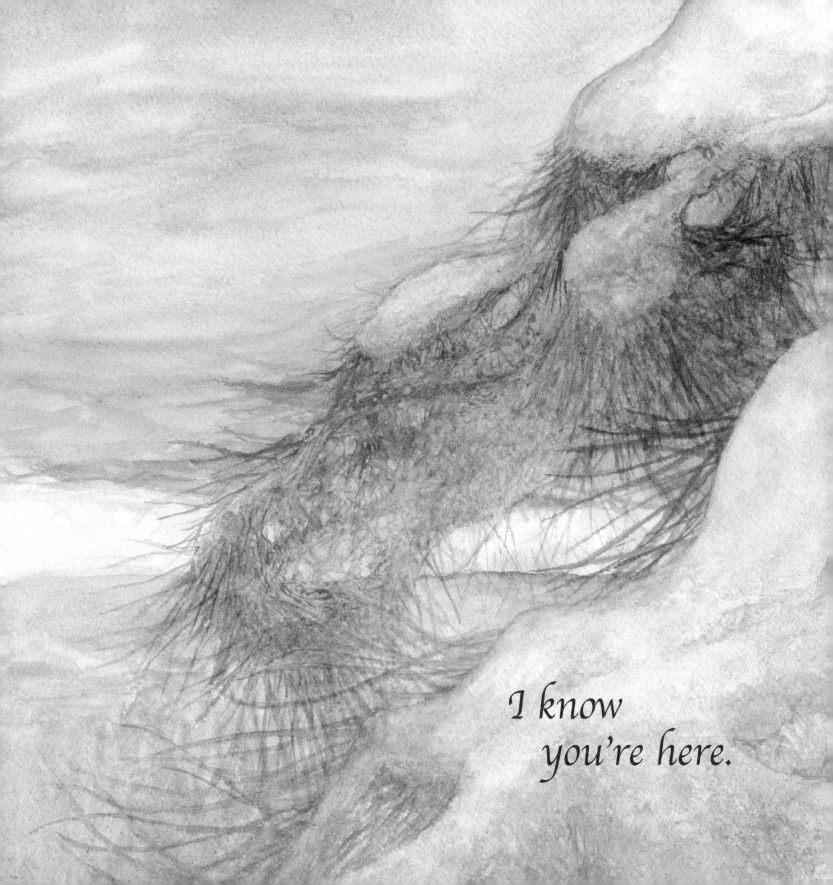

I know
you're here.

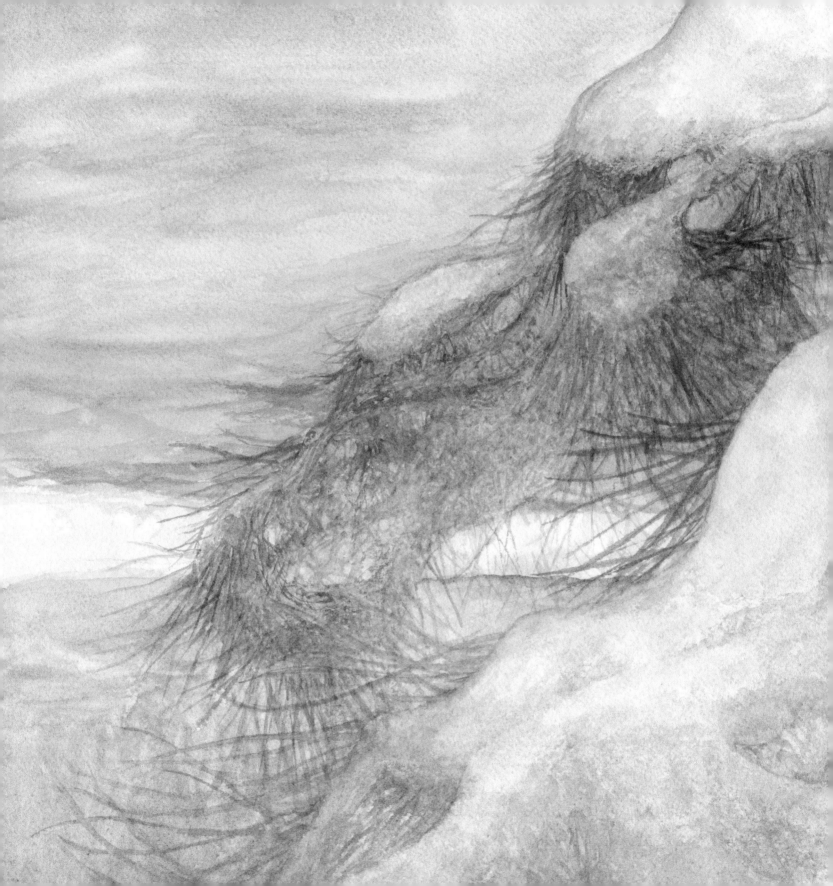

When the stars
twinkle in the
chilly night sky,

I know you're here.

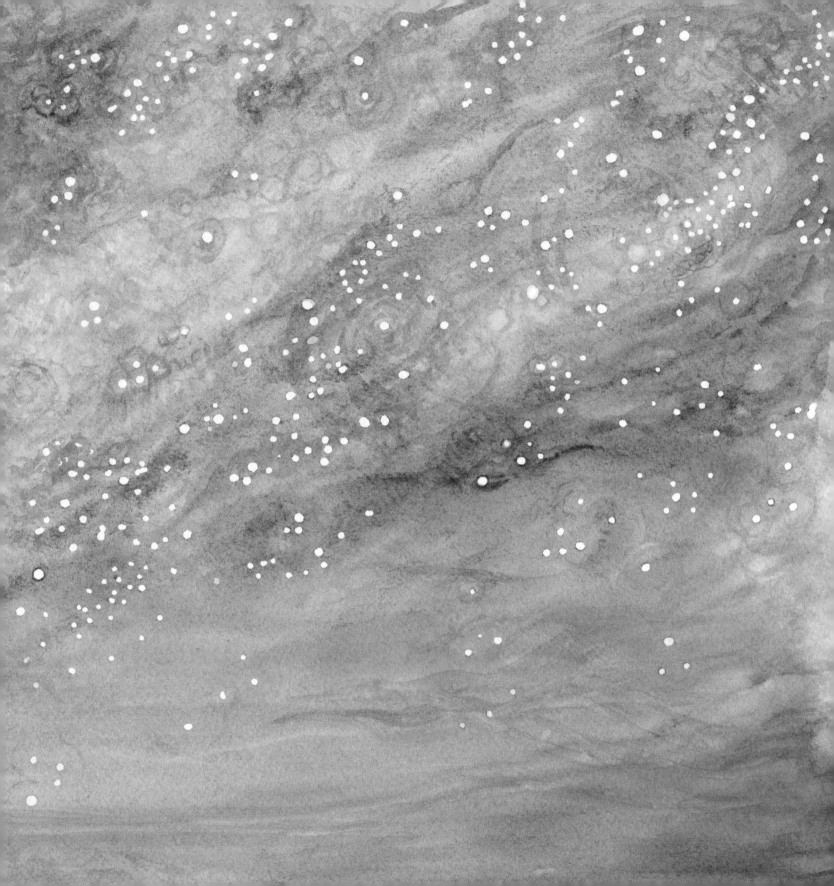

When the sun lifts its head
and brings hope of a new day,

I know you're here.

*In the blink
of an eye,
you were gone*

. . . but my heart knows

you're
really
here.

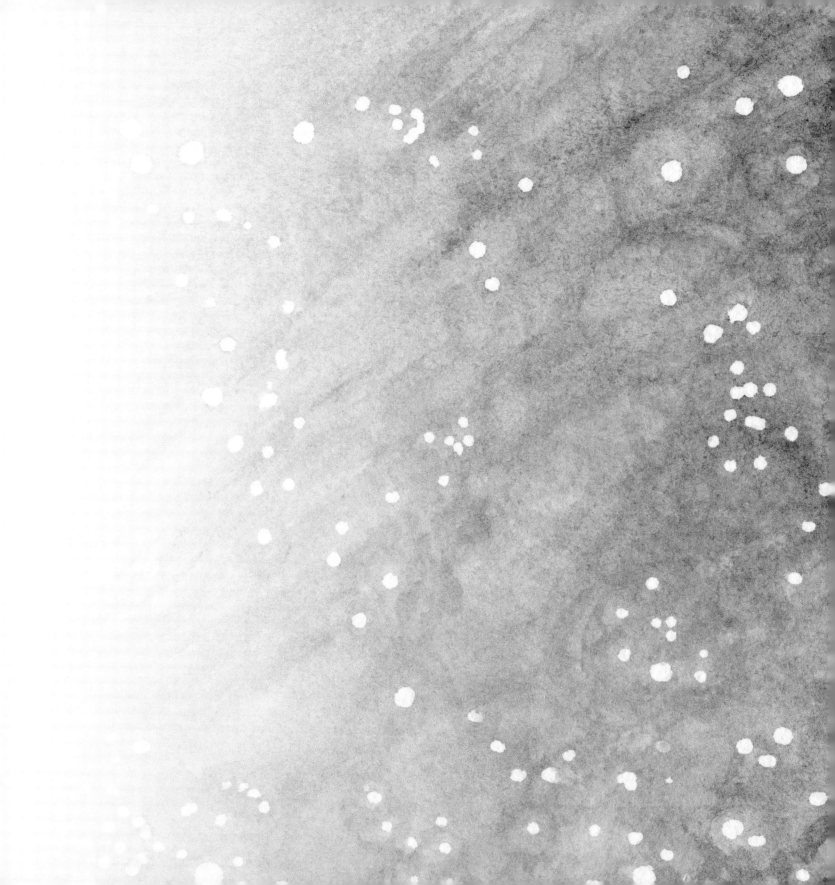

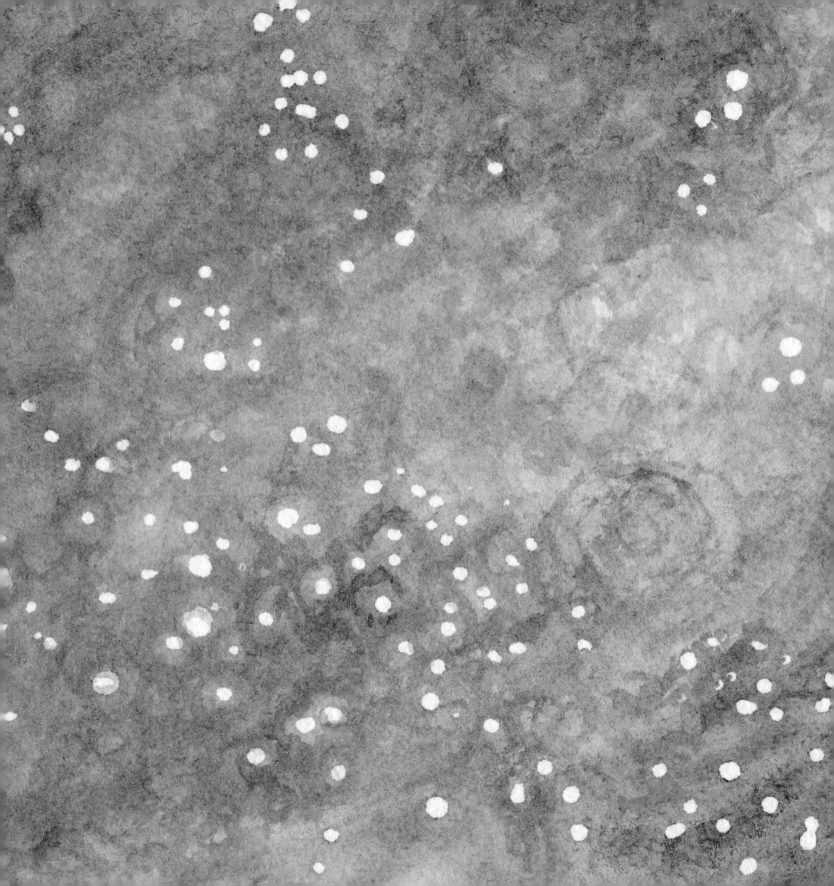